A Special Gift For

......................................................

With Love From

......................................................

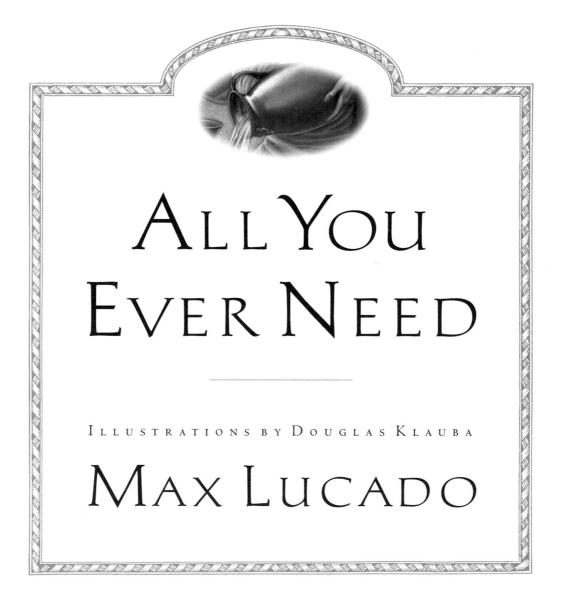

# ALL YOU EVER NEED

ILLUSTRATIONS BY DOUGLAS KLAUBA

## MAX LUCADO

CROSSWAY BOOKS • WHEATON, ILLINOIS

A DIVISION OF GOOD NEWS PUBLISHERS

*All You Ever Need*

Text copyright © 2000 by Max Lucado

Illustrations copyright © 2000 by Douglas Klauba

Published by Crossway Books, a division of Good News Publishers

1300 Crescent Street

Wheaton, Illinois 60187

Edited by Karen Hill

Design by David Uttley Design, Sisters, Oregon

First printing 2000

Printed in the United States of America

**Library of Congress Cataloging-in-Publication Data**

Lucado, Max.

    All you ever need/written by Max Lucado; illustrated by Douglas Klauba.

      p.  cm.

    Summary: A servant of the Watermaster, a kind man who gives water freely to the thirsty people of a desert village, tries to restrict this gift by imposing his own terms on it, even though his master wishes to share the water with all.

    ISBN 1-58134-134-2 (hardcover: aka. paper)

    [1. Generosity--Fiction.  2. Conduct of life--Fiction. 3. Parables.] I. Klauba, Douglas, ill. II. Title.

PZ7. L9684 An 2000

[Fic]--dc21                                          99-045155

                                                    CIP

| 15 | 14 | 13 | 12 | 11 | 10 | 09 | 08 | 07 | 06 | 05 | 04 | 03 | 02 | 01 | 00 |
| --- | --- | --- | --- | --- | --- | --- | --- | --- | --- | --- | --- | --- | --- | --- | --- |
| 15 | 14 | 13 | 12 | 11 | 10 | 9 | 8 | 7 | 6 | 5 | 4 | 3 | 2 | 1 | |

FOR BROOKE AND TARRYN

MAY YOU ALWAYS DRINK FROM GOD'S FOUNTAIN

Years ago there was a village in a desert land. In this dry land there was very little water. It seldom rained, but when it did, the people scurried about, capturing what they could in buckets and pots.

Every drop was like purest gold.

But even though the land was dry, the people were never thirsty.

For nearby lived a kind man named Tobias who owned a deep

wellspring from which poured clear, cool water.

The people called Tobias the "Watermaster," and they loved

him very much. He shared his treasure with everyone in the

village. All they had to do was ask, and the Watermaster

would gladly let them dip into his well.

"Drink all you want," he offered.

Not only did Tobias share from his well, but he taught his son to do this also. Tobias and his son, Julian, would help the people dip their buckets and carry their loads. Day after day, the people would come to the well.

Tobias would smile and say, "Take all you need."

He would talk to the people about their lives. He would laugh with them and inquire about their hopes and dreams, while Julian helped them draw water for their families.

Tobias was a kind friend, always ready to help the villagers.

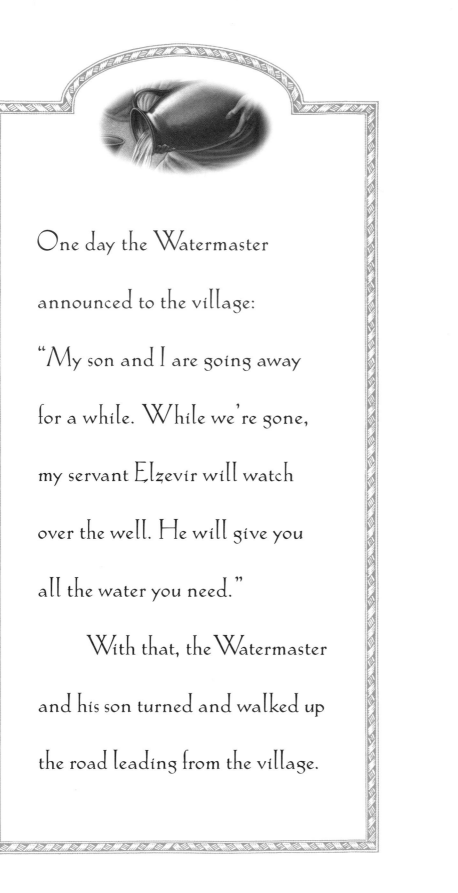

One day the Watermaster

announced to the village:

"My son and I are going away

for a while. While we're gone,

my servant Elzevir will watch

over the well. He will give you

all the water you need."

With that, the Watermaster

and his son turned and walked up

the road leading from the village.

The people were sad to see them leave, but they trusted Elzevir to supply their needs.

And, indeed, Elzevir did just as the Watermaster said.

Each day when the villagers came to ask for water, he eagerly filled their buckets.

As he did, he told the people, "Take all you need. There is plenty of water for all."

For a time, the village went about its business as usual.

But then one day, Elzevir noticed that the villagers were not grateful when they received their water. They just took their full buckets and raced away, without one word of thanks. This troubled Elzevir so much that he decided to stop giving water to everyone. He forgot the Watermaster's kindness to all.

Instead, he announced to the villagers: "From now on, I will not give water to those who aren't thankful."

The people were surprised. After Elzevir's announcement, all the villagers tried hard to remember to thank him when they received the water.

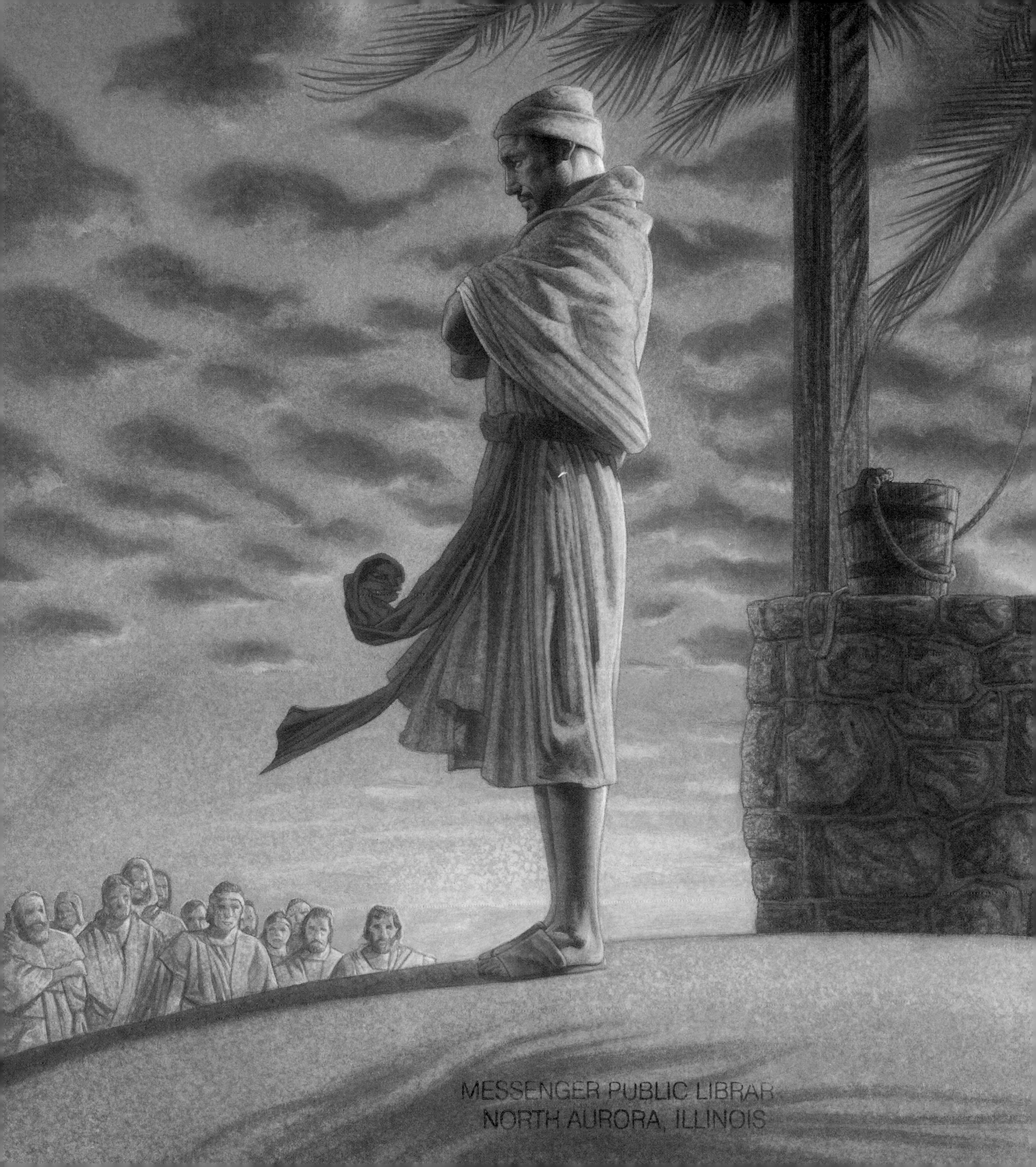

Some time later, Elzevir noticed that some of the people were unkind to their neighbors and mean to their animals. Again, the substitute Watermaster was bothered. He determined to give water only to nice people. "If you are mean to your animals or unkind to your neighbors, you will get no water," he announced.

The people worked hard to please Elzevir so they wouldn't go thirsty. But as time passed, the task master continued to find some new fault with the people. "You are too busy." "You are too lazy." "You're not quick enough—or smart enough—or pretty enough." With each decision, fewer people were given water.

Over time, the villagers grew sad and angry. "How can we ever

be good enough for Elzevir?" they questioned.

"We'll all die of thirst!" they cried.

As Elzevir's rules grew longer, the line for water grew

shorter. The people, growing thirsty, began to give up.

"It's no use," the people cried. "We can't please you."

In the midst of the shouting, a quiet figure approached the gathered villagers.

Elzevir eyed the man suspiciously. "Another thirsty soul, no doubt!" he growled. "Can you show that you are worthy of this water?"

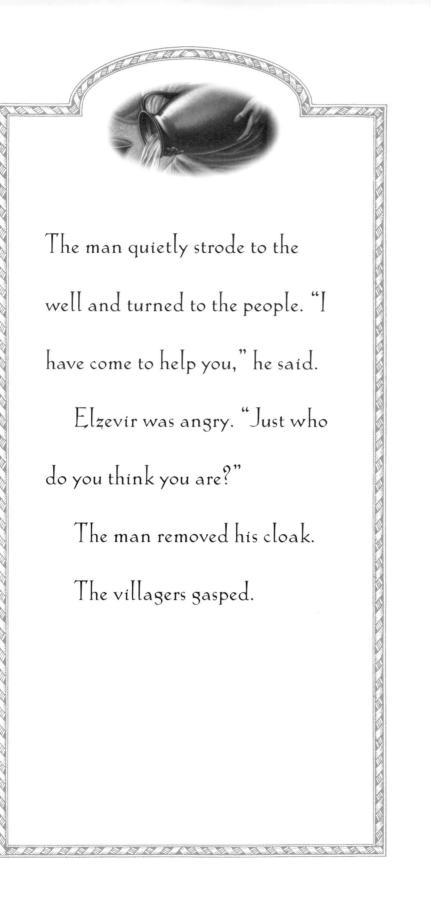

The man quietly strode to the
well and turned to the people. "I
have come to help you," he said.

Elzevir was angry. "Just who
do you think you are?"

The man removed his cloak.

The villagers gasped.

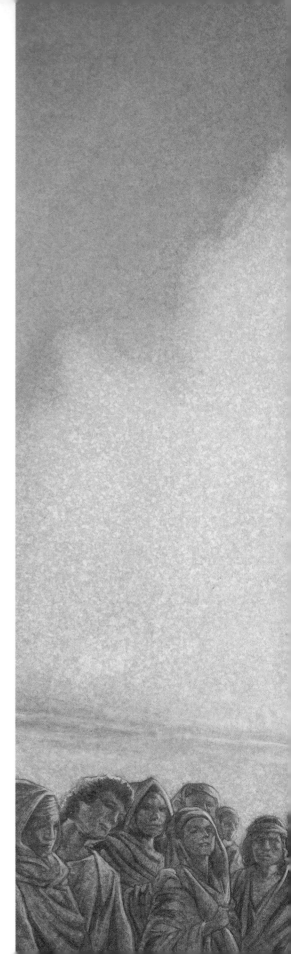

When they saw the familiar face, they began to whisper

among themselves.

"I am Julian, the Son of the Watermaster. My Father sent me

to share the water with all the people."

At that, the people cheered. Elzevir became afraid.

The villagers wanted revenge. "No water for Elzevir!" they shouted.

The Son held up his hand to the crowd, to quiet them.

"My Father's water is a gift to all," he said patiently.

"But Elzevir was cruel to us!"

"I know he was. But if water were given only to good people, who could drink?"

No one spoke.

The Son placed his hand on Elzevir's shoulder.

"Freely you have received, freely give."

The people looked at each other and were silent. They knew the Son's words were wise and true.

And so, from that day on, Elzevir was forgiven, and the water was shared freely.